SCHOOLS LIBRARY SERVICE

SCH This book belongs to...

D0358269

....

Note to parents and carers

Read it yourself is a series of classic, traditional tales, written in a simple way to give children a confident and successful start to reading.

Each book is carefully structured to include many high-frequency words that are vital for first reading. The sentences on each page are supported closely by pictures to help with reading, and to offer lively details to talk about.

The books are graded into four levels that progressively introduce wider vocabulary and longer stories as a reader's ability grows.

Ideas for use

- Begin by looking through the book and talking about the pictures. Has your child heard this story before?

- Help her with any words she does not know, either by helping her to sound them out or supplying them yourself.

- Developing readers can be concentrating so hard on the words that they sometimes don't fully grasp the meaning of what they're reading. Answering the puzzle questions on pages 30 and 31 will help with understanding

For more information and advice, visit www.ladybird.com/readityourself

Level 2 is ideal for children who have received some reading instruction and can read short, simple sentences with help.

Special features:

Frequent repetition of main story words and phrases

Short, simple sentences

The king and queen fell asleep, and everybody in the castle fell asleep.

Years went by and thorns grew on the castle.

Large, clear type

The prince cut down the thorns and went in the castle.

He looked at the sleeping princess.

"How beautiful she is!" he said.

Careful match between story and pictures

EAST SUSSEX SCHOOLS LIBRARY SERVICE	
13-Jul-2010	PETERS
1328539	

Educational Consultant: Geraldine Taylor

A catalogue record for this book is available from the British Library

Published by Ladybird Books Ltd
80 Strand, London, WC2R 0RL
A Penguin Company

2 4 6 8 10 9 7 5 3 1
© LADYBIRD BOOKS LTD MMX
Ladybird, Read It Yourself and the Ladybird Logo are registered or
unregistered trade marks of Ladybird Books Limited.

All rights reserved. No part of this publication may be reproduced,
stored in a retrieval system, or transmitted in any form or by any means,
electronic, mechanical, photocopying, recording or otherwise,
without the prior consent of the copyright owner.

ISBN: 978-1-40930-361-9

Printed in China

Sleeping Beauty

Illustrated by Richard Johnson

A king and queen had a baby girl. The good fairies came to see her.

"How beautiful she is!" they said.

The fairies cast spells for the baby princess.

"She will be kind," said one fairy.

"She will be clever," said another fairy.

8

9

Then, a bad fairy came in.
She looked at the
baby princess.

"How beautiful she is!"
said the bad fairy.

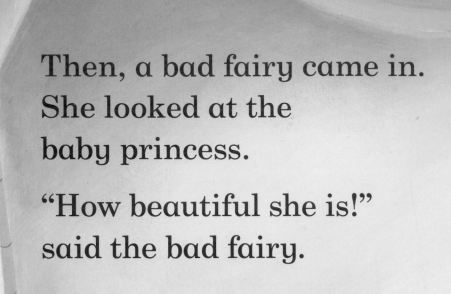

Then she cast a bad spell.

"The princess will prick
her finger and die!"
she said.

12

But then a good fairy
cast a spell.
"The princess will not die.
She will prick her finger
and fall asleep for
one hundred years."

14

Years went by and the
princess grew more kind
and more beautiful.

16

One day, the princess found a spinning wheel and pricked her finger.

She fell asleep.

18

The king and queen
fell asleep, and everybody
in the castle fell asleep.

Years went by and thorns
grew on the castle.

One hundred years
went by.

Then one day a prince
came to the castle.

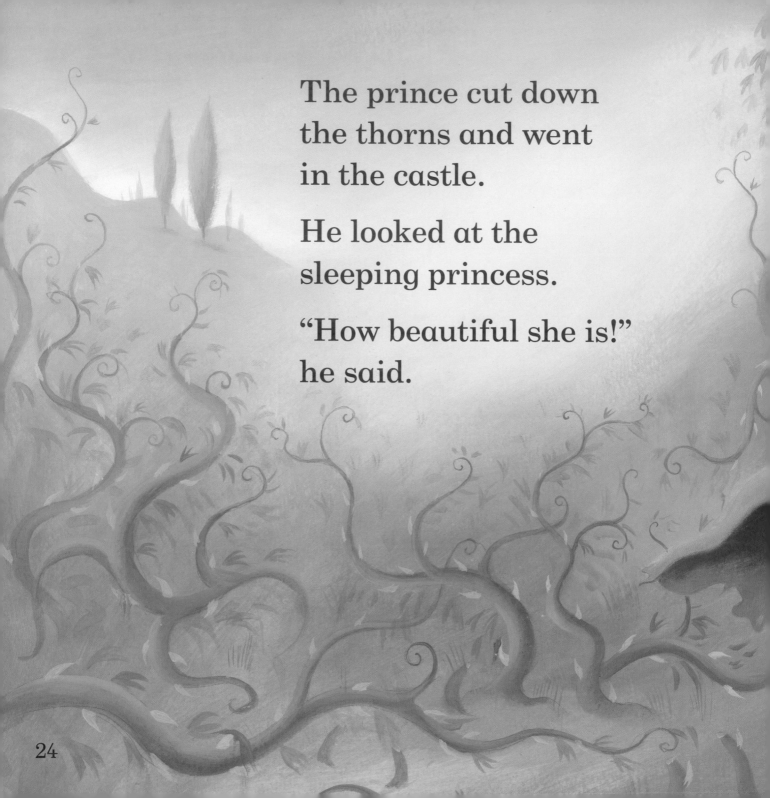

The prince cut down
the thorns and went
in the castle.

He looked at the
sleeping princess.

"How beautiful she is!"
he said.

The prince gave the sleeping princess a kiss and she woke up.

The king and queen woke up, and everybody in the castle woke up, too.

26

"Will you marry me?"
said the prince.

"Yes," said the princess.
So she did!

How much do you remember about the story of Sleeping Beauty? Answer these questions and find out!

- What spell does the bad fairy cast?

- What does Sleeping Beauty prick her finger on?

- How long does everyone fall asleep for?

- How does the prince wake up Sleeping Beauty?

Look at the pictures, then match them to the story words.

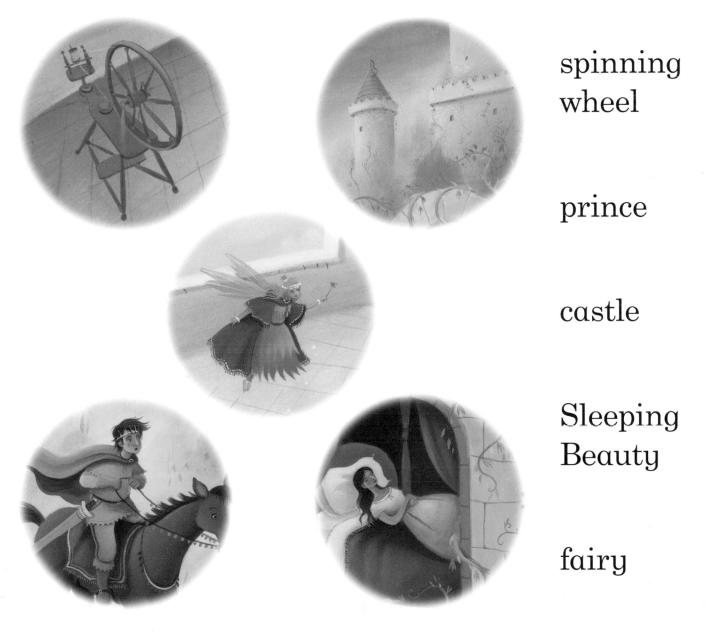

spinning
wheel

prince

castle

Sleeping
Beauty

fairy

Read it yourself
with Ladybird

The Three Billy Goats Gruff — Level 1

Cinderella — Level 1

Little Red Hen — Level 1

Goldilocks and the Three Bears — Level 1

The Magic Porridge Pot — Level 1

The Ugly Duckling — Level 1

The Gingerbread Man — Level 2

Sleeping Beauty — Level 2

Sly Fox and Red Hen — Level 2

The Three Little Pigs — Level 2

Town Mouse and Country Mouse — Level 2

Little Red Riding Hood — Level 2

The Elves and the Shoemaker — Level 3

Jack and the Beanstalk — Level 3

The Pied Piper of Hamelin — Level 4

The Wizard of Oz — Level 4

Collect all the titles in the series.